The Mouse Bride

A TALE FROM FINLAND

RETOLD AND ILLUSTRATED BY

LINDA ALLEN

PHILOMEL BOOKS ◆ NEW YORK

Copyright © 1992 by Linda Allen.   All rights reserved.
This book, or parts thereof, may not be reproduced in any
form without permission in writing from the publisher.
Philomel Books, a division of The Putnam & Grosset Book Group
200 Madison Avenue, New York, NY 10016
Published simultaneously in Canada.
Printed in Hong Kong by South China Printing Co. (1988) Ltd.
Book design by Gunta Alexander.   The text is set in Bembo.

Library of Congress Cataloging-in-Publication Data
Allen, Linda.   The mouse bride / by Linda Allen.   p.   cm.
Summary: Following the instructions of a wise old witch, a woodsman sends
his three sons to find wives but the youngest can only find a mouse.
[Folklore — Lapland.]   I. Title.   PZ8.1.A46Mo   1992
J 398.2 dc20   [E]   91-3948   CIP   AC   ISBN 0-399-22136-0

First Impression

To Marlowe

Once, in a country so far north that the sun shone much of the day, or not at all, there lived a woodsman called Pekka. Now, it was true that Pekka worried about each day and the days ahead, and so he went to an old Laplander woman who was known to tell fortunes, and asked her to tell him his.

She told him that he would have three sons, and she told him, "You must plant a tree for each who is born, and the tree you must name the same as the boy. When the boys are grown and wish to marry, each must cut down his name tree and follow in the direction it falls. Along that way, each will find his wife."

Knowing that there he would also find his own good fortune, Pekka did as the wise old woman told him. He planted a birch tree for his first son: Onni, he named him, and named the tree the same. For his second child, he planted an oak tree. He named the son Arne, and the tree the same. For his third and youngest son, he planted a fir tree, and Jukka was the name of the tree and the boy.

Now, the boys, they grew tall and sturdy, and the trees did as well. None in the forest, tree or boy, was more handsome. And then the day did come when the three sons came to Pekka: "Surely, Father, it is time for us to seek our wives."

And so Pekka told them about the wise old woman's words. "Follow the way the tree falls," he said. "It is the way to your own dear one." So each son chopped down his tree.

It happened that the tree of Onni, the eldest boy, fell to the ground pointing the way to a rich man's house. Arne's fell to the ground pointing to a farmer's house. The tree of Jukka, the youngest, sad to say, fell to the ground pointing to no neighbor at all, but rather to the deep, dark forest.

Each son set out by his tree's path to find his own dear one. But Jukka, of course, walked and walked and found nothing at all, neither house nor farm. Finally, after three days, he came to a clearing in the deepest part of the forest, and there he found a tiny *tupa* of gray logs.

"Is anyone here?" he said, and he knocked on the door. No one answered, so he lifted the latch to look inside. But he found the hut empty.

Empty, except there in the middle of the room on a table sat a little gray mouse with blue eyes and a white-tipped nose, looking right at him.

"Welcome to my house," the little mouse squeaked. "Why are you so sad?"

"I have my reasons," Jukka said. "I've traveled three days and three nights, and my bride is not at home!"

"Then, traveler, why don't you marry me?" the mouse twittered.

"Ka!" Jukka laughed. "Marry a mouse! Not me," he said.

"I promise, if you marry me," the little mouse said, "you will never be sorry for the bargain."

"Ka! I'm sure I couldn't be worse off than I am right now!"

The mouse began to dance all around the table on her little gray feet. "Then you and I have a bargain," she said happily. "Go now. I'll be waiting for you when you come back." Nor did she stop dancing.

But the moment Jukka closed the door and began his journey back through the woods, he was sad again, for what would his father and brothers say!

"Did you find your own dear one, then?" they asked, when they first saw him.

"I found a fine wife, indeed," Jukka said.

"Tell us about her," they said.

"I can tell you only that her eyes are blue and her nose is white."

"Blue eyes and a white nose!" the brothers jeered, and they began to laugh.

When Onni and Arne bragged all night long of their good luck and the wonderful wives they had found, poor Jukka only sat silent, and finally went to bed.

At dawn the next day Pekka said to each of his sons, "Today you must go and bring me back something that your bride has baked. A loaf of bread is what I want."

Off Onni and Arne set, happily and quickly, to their new brides. But Jukka trudged slowly through the forest to his little gray mouse.

Again, when he opened the door, his mouse bride was sitting on the table. "What do you want, my dear one," she asked, "or are you here to marry me?"

"My father has sent me for some of your own bread," he said, thinking it was impossible. "Could you make me a loaf?"

"Yes, I can," said the little mouse bride, and she took in her paws the tiny reindeer bell that sat next to her on the table, and began to ring it. *Ring a ding. Ring a ding.* At the sound, a thousand mice came into the room, all dancing on their toes.

"Bring me the finest grain that you can find," she said to them. "And hurry."

Away they all scampered, and before the clock had struck the next hour, they had all come back. Each carried a single grain of the finest wheat, which the little gray mouse took, ground up, and made into a loaf of bread.

It was a wonder to Jukka that a mouse could do this, but he asked no questions. He only thanked the little mouse, placed the loaf under his arm, and started home.

It was a fine loaf of rye bread from his bride that Onni set on his father's table. Arne's loaf was barley, and good enough. But Pekka's eyes grew wide when he saw that Jukka's loaf was baked large and firm, and of the finest wheat flour.

At dawn the next day Pekka said to his sons, "Bring me a piece of cloth woven by your dear one. I wish to see who is the most clever with her hands."

Each son went his way again. Again, when he arrived at the tupa, Jukka found the little mouse in the middle of the table.

"Do you seek something from me, dear one, or have you come to marry me?"

"My father has sent me to fetch a piece of cloth that you have woven with your hands," Jukka said, thinking she could never do this. "Can you weave it for me?"

"That will take only a little while!" the mouse bride cried, and again she rang the tiny reindeer bell. Once again the thousand mice danced into the room on their toes.

"Find me the finest shreds of flax," she said. "There's not a minute to waste!"

Away the thousand mice scampered, and in a moment they all were back in the room, each with a shred of the finest white flax.

"Now we will weave it together," said the mouse bride.

And that is what they did. Some carded the flax, others spun it, and the little gray mouse herself wove it. Before the clock had struck the next hour, the piece of cloth was finished. The mouse bride folded the cloth and tucked it into a nutshell, which she put into Jukka's hand. He thanked her kindly and hurried home.

His father and his brothers were waiting for him. Onni showed the others his square of cloth; it was coarse and stiff. Arne's bride had woven her cloth; it was loose and uneven. Then Pekka asked to see Jukka's cloth.

"There is so little of it, there's not enough to show," Jukka said, and he took the tiny nutshell from his pocket.

Onni and Arne burst out laughing. But their father took the little nutshell in his hand and drew out the cloth farther and farther. The cloth had been so finely woven that yards and yards had been folded there.

A few days after, Pekka called his sons together again. "It is summer now. Go and fetch your brides. I wish to see which of you has made the wisest choice. You shall all wed on Midsummer's Day!"

So joyful were Onni and Arne, they fairly ran down the paths to get their wives, but not poor Jukka. He didn't know what to do. He started through the woods like a man walking in a bad dream.

At the tupa, there was the little gray mouse waiting.

"Come with me," he said glumly. "My father wants to meet you."

"Ka! We will go together," she sang in her tiny, sweet voice. Then she rang her reindeer bell. This time five sleek mice danced into the room, pulling a carriage made of a chestnut burr, with a toadstool for a roof.

Gracefully, the mouse bride climbed up and sat in the tiny carriage, as proud as any queen.

Jukka cried out, "What will my father say when he sees you? And my brothers, they will laugh when they see how small you are."

"Don't be afraid," the little mouse said. "Do as I tell you, dear Jukka, and I promise you will be a happy man."

The five mice started off at a quick pace, pulling the carriage through the lane, with Jukka walking beside them. He did not know whether to laugh or cry.

They were crossing a bridge on the third day of their journey, the mice moving at a quick trot, when they met a peasant boy. He had a hard, ugly face and big shoulders.

"Get out of my way!" he growled.

Before Jukka could stop him, the peasant boy kicked the tiny chestnut-burr carriage, carrying the little mouse bride right over the side of the bridge and into the river. Splash! They disappeared.

Jukka himself was ready to fight the boy, but when he turned around the boy was gone. So he turned back to the running water again, and saw an amazing thing: five sleek gray horses drawing a golden carriage were climbing out of the river and up the bank. In the carriage, holding the reins, sat—not a little gray mouse—but a delicate young maiden.

"Are you coming with me?" the maiden asked. Jukka, feeling quite stupid, just rubbed his eyes.

"Don't you know me, dear one?" she asked. "I am your mouse bride. Ride here beside me, where you belong."

And Jukka climbed into the carriage alongside the pretty maiden, took the reins in his own hands, and she told him her story. She had been a king's daughter, but when she was fifteen, a Lapland witch, jealous of her beauty, changed her and all her servants into gray mice.

The spell could be broken only if one young man asked to marry her and another tried to kill her by casting her into the water.

"You, Jukka," she said, "asked me to marry you, and the peasant lad kicked me into the water and tried to drown me. So now the spell is broken, and I am my own true self once more!"

Jukka was the happiest man in all the world. "And what shall I call you when my father asks your name?"

"You shall call me Olga, for that is my name," said his bride.

"Then, Olga, my own sweetheart," Jukka said, "it is Midsummer's Eve and we must hurry home for our wedding feast. The village folk will be there, and we will dance all day and all the night."

As before, Onni and Arne had returned home first. But this time when Jukka came they waited for him with their brides. You can imagine how they felt when they saw Jukka driving through the woods in a golden carriage with five handsome horses. They could not believe their eyes.

And when they saw Jukka's wife, they could not speak, for she was the most beautiful woman they had ever seen.

So the three sons were married in their father's house, there in the woods. It was decked with green boughs and flowers of every kind, and the village musician came and played on his kantele and sang while all the young people danced all night by the moonlight. Old Pekka was that happy to see his sons and daughters so happy, and he knew what his good fortune was.

When the musician played the last tune, and the sun began to climb in the sky, Jukka and Olga climbed into the carriage once again, and the five gray horses took them back swiftly to the valley hidden in the trees from where they had come. But the tiny gray tupa was gone!

In its place was a great stone castle.

"Ah," said Olga and she smiled. "Now, it is as it was when I was a child, before the old Laplander woman worked her witchcraft on me."

And there it was, far from the village, in the hidden woods, that Jukka and his mouse bride lived happily ever after.